Owl All Alone

Lucy Daniels

With special thanks to Tabitha Jones
For Isla Rose and Ava Violet Hawkins
Illustrations by Jo Anne Davies for Artful Doodlers

ORCHARD BOOKS

First published in Great Britain in 2020 by The Watts Publishing Group

1 3 5 7 9 10 8 6 4 2

Text copyright © Working Partners, 2020
Illustrations copyright © Working Partners, 2020

The moral rights of the author and illustrator have been asserted.

A CIP catalogue record for this book
is available from the British Library.

ISBN 978 1 40835 927 3

Printed and bound in Great Britain by Clays Ltd, Elcograf S.p.A

The paper and board used in this book are made from wood from responsible sources.

CONTENTS

CHAPTER ONE

Amelia stood up and pushed her hair back from her face. She felt hot and sweaty from digging in the morning sun, and her arms ached, but she let out a contented sigh. "Do you think this will be deep enough?" she asked.

Her friend Izzy stood nearby, holding

a lavender plant. Clusters of little purple petals seemed to explode out from the green stems. "I think so," Izzy said.

Amelia stood back, letting the breeze cool her skin while Izzy planted the lavender into the hole.

"Good job!" said Miss Hafiz, Amelia's teacher. She was returning from the water butt with an overflowing watering can. "This garden's really taking shape!"

Amelia smiled as she gazed around the school's small plot. Leaves and twigs littered the grass from a storm the night before. But even so, the place looked transformed. Amelia and her classmates had cleared the weeds from around

patches of geraniums and peonies, and fragrant flowers and shrubs now filled the newly dug beds.

"What a good idea it was to create a wildlife garden, Amelia," Miss Hafiz said. "And it's kind of you both to give up some of your half-term to come and finish the work."

A warm glow of pride spread through Amelia. "I can't wait until it's finished!" she said. "We should get all sorts of birds and insects."

"I never really thought of gardening before," Izzy said. Her cheeks were flushed as she got to her feet. "But with the whole village working on their gardens for the Welford Gardening Competition, it's like the latest craze!"

"Especially this year," Miss Hafiz

said, "with all the buzz the TV show is creating. You can hardly go outdoors without bumping into a camera crew filming someone's flowerbeds!"

Excitement bubbled inside Amelia as she thought of the show. "I can't believe they're going to dedicate a whole episode of *Blooming Brilliant* to the gardening competition!"

Izzy giggled. "Although it's kind of scary too. I keep thinking I'll walk past a camera without noticing and end up on telly wearing some goofy expression."

"Well, you're safe in here," Miss Hafiz said. "Look – the bees have already found your lavender!" She pointed

 towards a pair
of honey bees
buzzing around
the purple flowers. "How about we rake
up the leaves from the storm last night?"

Amelia checked her watch. "Uh-oh!"
she said. "I'm supposed to be meeting
Sam up at Brambledown Hall.
We promised Kasia we'd help set up
for filming."

"Don't worry – Izzy and I will finish
up here," Miss Hafiz said. "You've done
so much already, Amelia!"

When Amelia reached Brambledown

Hall, she found the long, sweeping driveway full of cars. People hurried about pushing large black cases on trolleys across the gravel. *Film equipment*, guessed Amelia. *The crew are setting up!*

The heavy wooden doors to Brambledown stood open. Inside the entrance hall, more darkly clad film technicians were busy running cables over the black and white tiles. Amelia heard the low hum of voices coming from the ballroom and carefully picked her way over the cables and down a corridor.

In the ballroom, she found engineers rigging cameras in front of long tables

covered with pots of flowers and shrubs.
Sam was busy lifting more pots from a
cart and adding them to the display.

"I was starting to think you weren't
coming!" Sam said, grinning as Amelia
joined him. "Bernard's arriving soon, and
we've still got all of those to put out for
the next round of judging." Sam gestured

towards the
cart of plants.

Amelia
took a fuchsia
with bobbing
heart-shaped
flowers from
the cart and

placed it on the table
beside a pot of peonies.

"Hey there!" said
a familiar voice from
behind her. Amelia turned
to see Kasia Kaminski
striding towards them,
smartly dressed in a black
suit with chunky silver
jewellery. Kasia was the sister of Julia, the
receptionist at Animal Ark. She was also
the organiser of the whole gardening
competition. "These plants look great,"
Kasia said. "Let me help you finish. It's
not long until they start filming."

"How's Blossom doing?" asked

Amelia, as Kasia picked up a huge lily, with glossy leaves sticking out in every direction. Amelia and Sam had recently helped Kasia's little puppy to sleep peacefully at night.

"Oh, just great," said Kasia with a smile. "Thanks to you two!" She set the lily down and frowned slightly. "This one looks a little windswept," she said.

Sam nodded. "Some of the plants got knocked over by the storm last night. I've tried to tidy them up."

Kasia smoothed the leaves of the lily, making them all stand tall. Then she gave a satisfied nod.

"How's the school garden doing?" Sam

asked Amelia as they unloaded more plant pots.

"Great!" Amelia said. "We planted loads of lavender today."

"I heard about Amelia's plan for a wildlife garden!" Kasia said. "It's such a good idea. What other plants are you putting in? I might be able to suggest some."

But Amelia was too surprised to answer. She frowned, peering into a particularly large plant on the trolley. It had reddish-orange flowers that looked like butterflies. But it wasn't the flowers that had caught her attention.

Something fluffy was nestled in the

17

foliage at the base of the plant – some
sort of animal, all covered in tufty greyish
brown fur. *No, not fur,* Amelia realised as
the creature turned a pair of big, round
eyes up towards her. *Feathers!*

"Look!" Amelia whispered, bending
closer. "It's a baby owl!" The owlet
shuffled back anxiously, pressing itself
against the plant's woody stem. Then it

made a soft little
clicking noise
with its beak.
Oh – it's so little!
Amelia thought.
*What's it doing
here on its own?*

CHAPTER TWO

Sam drew in a sharp breath of surprise.

"My goodness!" Kasia whispered.

Suddenly, Amelia noticed a dark stain of blood on one of the owlet's stubby wings. "It's hurt!" she said.

"Maybe it fell out of its nest," Sam suggested.

Kasia glanced up at the ballroom ceiling, as if half expecting to see a nest there, then shook her head. "But how on earth did it get into the pot plant?"

The owl blinked up at them. It tried to shuffle further into the shadows of the plant, but it had nowhere to go. It opened its beak and let out a fierce little hiss, showing a pointed triangle of tongue. Then it flapped its stumpy wings and gave an angry squawk.

"The poor little thing!" Amelia said.

"I think we should call Animal Ark."

Kasia nodded and pulled her phone from her pocket. "Let me call Julia now." After speaking a few words in Polish to her sister, Kasia held out the phone to Amelia. "Julia says Mrs Hope would like to speak to you."

Amelia took the phone.

"I hear you've found an owlet," Mrs Hope said.

"Yes, in a pot plant at Brambledown Hall," Amelia explained. "It's not got real feathers yet, just fluff, and one of its wings is injured."

"Can you tell me what it looks like?" Mrs Hope said. "Is it white or brown?"

Amelia peered again at the little owl. It had half closed its eyes now, and tucked its tufty head into its body, almost like it was trying to disappear. "It's neither really," Amelia said. "It's kind of grey with bits of brown."

"In that case it sounds like a very young tawny owlet," Mrs Hope said. "Normally I would say we need to leave it by its nest. But if it's injured, I think you'd better bring it in for a check-up first."

"Won't the mother bird reject it if we touch it?" Amelia asked.

"No," Mrs Hope said. "Tawny owls don't have much sense of smell, so

handling their young is fine, but be careful. Even though it's little, the owlet's claws will still be sharp. Wrap it up in something to protect your hands and cover its head so it doesn't get stressed."

Amelia thanked Mrs Hope and handed Kasia back her phone. "We need to take the baby owl to Animal Ark," Amelia told Kasia. "Can someone give us a lift?"

Kasia nodded. "Let me sort something out," she said, and hurried away.

"Mrs Hope said we should wrap it up," Amelia told Sam. She shrugged off her hoodie, draped it over her hands, and knelt beside the little owl. As Amelia gently eased both hands under the owl's

body, it let out a sharp squawk, and flapped its wings. "It's OK, I've got you," Amelia said. She lifted the owlet into the crook of her arm and looped a fold of fabric over its head. The little bird settled down at once.

"Don't worry," Amelia told it softly. "We're going to look after you."

"Thank you so much!" Amelia said a

short while later, as she climbed out of
Janie Dunn's Land Rover outside Animal
Ark. The local farmer had kindly agreed
to give them a lift. Janie waved goodbye,
and Amelia and Sam hurried into the
surgery, Amelia cradling the wrapped-up
owl in her arms.

"Mr Hope is waiting for you," Julia
told them from her desk. "Go right on
through."

Sam held the door to the assessment
room open, and Amelia carried the owl
inside.

"Let's see what we've got then," Mr
Hope said. He gently took the owlet
from Amelia and unwrapped it from

her hoodie. The little creature started scolding and flapping at once, but with deft movements, Mr Hope circled its legs and wing-tips with his fingers and laid it back along his forearm. The owl stopped screeching, but its saucer-like eyes followed Mr Hope's every movement.

First Mr Hope ran his free hand up the bird's fluffy body, feeling around its chest, then back down again, gently pressing its

tummy. He checked the owl's scaly legs for injuries, then shone a light into each eye. Next, he extended first the owlet's good wing, then the injured one. Finally, he wrapped the little owl back up in Amelia's hoodie.

"It seems a little underfed," Mr Hope said. "There are some abrasions to the wing, but they should heal well enough on their own. The fact it's so feisty is definitely a good sign. It's just as well you found it when you did. It couldn't have survived long on its own."

"How do you think it hurt its wing?" Sam asked.

Mr Hope shrugged. "It's hard to say.

Possibly a predator attacked it, or it may have got caught up in the high winds last night. Young tawny owls start venturing away from the nest quite young, but at this age, they still rely on their parents to feed them."

"So, what do we do now?" Amelia asked.

"We need to find its nest," Mr Hope said. "I'm afraid it wouldn't survive on its own, but if its parents are still there, they'll take care of it. Mrs Hope will take you back to the hall to look for the nest while I give this little one some fluids."

"What if we can't find the nest?" Sam asked anxiously.

Mr Hope looked grave, and Amelia felt her stomach twist with fear. "We'll have to cross that bridge if we come to it," he said. "But it could certainly make things tough for this little guy. We'd better keep our fingers crossed."

CHAPTER THREE

Back in the ballroom at Brambledown
Hall, every table was groaning under
the weight of colourful plants. A young
man with blue hair, wearing a *Blooming
Brilliant* sweatshirt, was just wheeling
a cart away from the final table.
Amelia and Sam hurried towards him,

leading Mrs Hope.

"Wait!" Sam called as they neared the man. He turned, showing piercings in his nose and lip, and all the way up both ears.

"Everything all right?" the man asked.

"Can you please show us where the pot plants were kept before they were brought into the ballroom?" Amelia said.

"Were they stored outdoors, by any chance?" Mrs Hope added.

The young man looked puzzled but

nodded. He pointed to a pair of double doors that led to the grounds. "There's a big beech tree outside. We kept all the pots under it while another segment of the show was being filmed."

"Can we take a look?" Amelia asked.

"We found a baby owl in one of the pots," Sam explained. "We need to find its nest."

"Oh, wow!" the man said, grinning suddenly. "I'll give you a hand. My name's Craig, and I'm a big fan of birds of prey." Leaving his cart where it was, Craig led Sam, Amelia and Mrs Hope out on to the veranda, then down on to the lawn.

"There it is," Craig said, pointing. The beech tree stood not far from the house, its wide branches laden with pretty green leaves.

They all circled the tree's gnarled trunk, looking up into the branches. Though Amelia could see every twig and leaf outlined clearly against the bright blue sky, she couldn't spot anything that looked like a nest.

"I don't see any owls," Sam said, echoing her thoughts.

"The nest would be hidden in the crook of a branch, or inside a knot hole," Mrs Hope said.

This might not even be the right place, thought Amelia, feeling desperate. Brambledown Estate had thousands of trees. How would they ever find the nest?

"Ew! Look out," said Sam, shuffling away. "Fox poo!"

Amelia glanced down and saw a small dark blob near her boot. Then she noticed tiny, pale rib-bones in it, and part of a little skull poking from what looked like mangy fur.

"I don't think that's fox poo," she said.

Mrs Hope bent down and looked closely at what Sam had found. "You're right," she said. "It's an owl pellet. Made of all the stuff they can't digest. They spit it out after a meal."

"So there *is* a nest here!" said Amelia, her heart swelling hopefully.

"It seems so," said Mrs Hope. "But we can't leave our owlet here unless we know it's the right place. We need to take a proper look in the branches."

Sam ran his eyes up the beech tree's broad trunk. "I might be able to climb it," he said.

"It's too dangerous," said Mrs Hope.

36

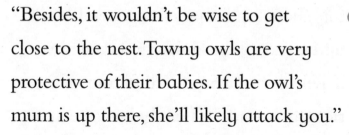

"Besides, it wouldn't be wise to get close to the nest. Tawny owls are very protective of their babies. If the owl's mum is up there, she'll likely attack you."

Craig frowned thoughtfully. "Do you have a mobile phone with you?" he asked Mrs Hope.

The vet nodded. "I do, but why?"

"I think I might be able to help," Craig said. "Wait here a moment. I'll be back!"

Before long, Craig returned from the ballroom, carrying a silver ladder under one arm, and a long black pole.

"I was thinking that if we got our phones linked up on a video call," he told Mrs Hope, "I could use this to lift

my phone up into the branches. It's just an extendable pole from a boom mic. Then we can take a virtual tour of the treetop!"

"That's a brilliant idea!" Amelia said.

"It sounds like it might work," said Mrs Hope. "But you'll have to be careful not to drop your phone!"

"Don't worry," Craig said. "I do this sort of thing all the time. I'm a film student as well as a runner for the show."

Once Mrs Hope had tapped Craig's phone number into her mobile, Craig quickly set up his makeshift wildlife camera. He set the ladder against the tree and started to climb, with his phone

clipped securely to the
black pole. While Mrs
Hope held the bottom
of the ladder, Sam
and Amelia crowded
around the wavering
picture on her phone.

"Hang on!" Craig
called down. "I'm just
getting the camera up
into the branches."

At first, all Amelia could make out was blurry tree bark. But then the picture stabilised, and Amelia spotted an untidy bundle of sticks and dry grass in the crook of a branch. The branch itself had broken and was hanging at an angle. White droppings and feathers covered the tatty nest, but there was no sign of any owls.

"Can you see anything?" Craig called down to them.

Amelia and Sam exchanged worried looks.

"We can see a nest," Amelia said. "But it

looks broken up, and it's empty."

Amelia showed the phone to Mrs Hope, and she let out a sigh. "You're right," she said. "The owls must have abandoned the nest after the branch snapped." She raised her voice. "Thanks, Craig. You'd better come down."

Craig looked as glum as Amelia felt as he reached the ground. "It was really windy last night," he said. "I guess that's what caused the damage. But I suppose this means your little owl has no home to go back to."

Amelia felt suddenly cold. *Mr Hope said the chick won't survive without its parents …* "Can't we hand-rear it?" she asked.

41

Mrs Hope shook her head. "Baby owls are really tricky. There are even laws about who can look after them and for how long. If you don't get it right, they can't be reintroduced to the wild." She sighed. "We'll have to find a specialist sanctuary to take it. In the meantime, I'm going to ask the head gardener at Brambledown to look out for tawny

owls. If there were more young in the nest, the adults might have found a new nesting site nearby. It's possible we might be able to reunite our chick with its family."

Amelia thought of the poor little owlet. "I hope we do find them!" she murmured.

CHAPTER FOUR

Excited chatter filled the school garden. A gusty wind carried the smell of churned earth and summer flowers as Sam and Amelia stood together with their classmates, waiting for Miss Hafiz to speak. Their teacher had called everyone's parents the night before,

asking the class to come in the next day.
Amelia could hardly stand still, she was
so eager to find out why.

Finally, Miss Hafiz clapped her hands
and everyone fell silent.

"Thank you all for coming in on your
half-term," Miss Hafiz said. "I have some
news! *Blooming Brilliant* have asked to do
a segment of the show from the school
garden. They want to interview students
from our class to find out about the great

work you've been doing here!"

Caleb let out a whoop, and everyone started talking at once. Amelia's heart raced with excitement. *The wildlife garden was my idea and now it's going to be on TV!* She gave Sam a nudge, and he grinned, his eyes shining.

Miss Hafiz raised a hand for quiet. "Now I know you've all worked hard, and you should be proud of yourselves, but I'm afraid the show won't be able to feature the whole class, although we've all been invited to watch the filming." A few worried glances passed between the students. Mrs Hafiz went on. "So, Bernard Bloom is coming to select two students to represent all of you."

"Hello!" A deep voice rang out across the playground. Amelia turned to see Bernard Bloom striding towards them, smiling and waving. He was wearing a navy blazer and a cravat printed with red roses. At the same moment, a sharp elbow jabbed Amelia as her classmate Tiffany pushed past. Looking smart in a white summer dress, Tiffany opened the garden gate for the TV presenter and held out her hand. Bernard Bloom swept his floppy blond hair aside and shook it.

"Pleased to meet you … er … ?"

"My name's Tiffany Banks. Welcome to our Wildlife Garden!" She gestured through the gate and stepped aside for Bernard to enter.

"This is wonderful!" Bernard said, blue eyes twinkling as he smiled at them. "I hope you don't mind if I look around."

"Of course!" Tiffany said brightly.
"Why not start over here, where we've
put up new nesting boxes?"

Amelia rolled her eyes. *Typical Tiffany,
acting like she did everything when she never
even got her hands dirty!* But she pushed
her irritation aside. Her classmates
quickly spread out across the garden, all
watching Bernard eagerly as he started
his tour.

Sam stationed himself near the bee

hotel he'd made from bamboo sticks. Amelia chose to stay close to the flowerbeds she'd planted with Izzy. She did her best to keep smiling while Tiffany led Bernard around, practically tugging him by his sleeve and laughing at everything he said. *She's treating this like an audition!* thought Amelia.

As Bernard neared Sam's bee hotel, Amelia crossed her fingers, then grinned as the TV host stopped. Sam answered

the presenter's questions enthusiastically, gesturing with his arms as he spoke.

Next, Bernard asked Izzy about the water butt collecting run-off rain water from the shed roof. After a couple more stops, he headed towards Amelia's flowerbeds. Amelia's heart thundered in her chest as he stopped and smiled at her. "What a colourful display," he said. "How did you decide what to plant?"

Amelia felt herself blush, but as she started to speak, her nerves vanished. "We chose plants for the garden that provide food and shelter for insects, and we made sure to pick shrubs that bloom and fruit at different times of year, so there

is always something for the insects and birds."

Bernard nodded with approval. "I couldn't have chosen a better mix myself," he said. Then he moved on, leaving Amelia almost bursting with pride.

Finally, Bernard clapped his hands together loudly. "Right then everybody, gather round," he said. Once the class had assembled before him, Bernard went on. "Thank you all for your help. It really is wonderful to see so many young gardening enthusiasts. You've made my decision a very tricky one, but I've made up my mind."

Amelia found herself holding her breath. At her side, Sam leaned forwards.

After a pause that seemed to last for ever, Bernard finally continued. "First, I'd like to invite Sam to be on the show," the presenter said. Amelia gave her friend's arm a squeeze, and he shot her a grin.

"Without Sam's enthusiasm, telling me all about your garden at his parents' bed and breakfast, where I'm staying, I would never

have known it was here — or how much
it means to you all.

"The second person I'd like to invite
on to the programme is a young lady
who's shown herself to be confident and
keen — a natural presenter, in fact ..."
Amelia bunched her fists, her body tense.
"Tiffany!" Bernard said.

Amelia let out her breath in a
disappointed rush, while Tiffany beamed
proudly. Amelia clapped along with her
classmates, but she couldn't help thinking
it wasn't fair. *Tiffany hardly worked on the
garden at all!*

"You should have been chosen instead
of me!" Sam whispered in her ear. "The

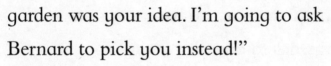

garden was your idea. I'm going to ask
Bernard to pick you instead!"

Amelia shook her head fiercely. "No!"
she said. "You deserve it as much as
anyone."

"This way, Sam and Tiffany," Miss
Hafiz said, gesturing for them to follow
her. "Everyone else, thank you so much
for coming."

Sam shot Amelia an apologetic smile,
then turned to join Tiffany as she strode
past.

"I knew I'd be picked!" Tiffany told
Sam, tossing her hair. "As Bernard said,
I'm a natural!"

For a moment, Amelia stood still,

feeling deflated. But then she squared her shoulders. *Tiffany is really good at public speaking. And at least Sam is going to be on TV ...*

She tried to put it from her mind. There were more important things to worry about at Animal Ark!

When Amelia reached the surgery, she found the waiting room heaving. Every seat was taken, and she could see animal carriers of all different shapes and sizes.

"It's so busy!" Amelia said to Julia. "I was hoping to visit the baby owl, but is there anything I can help with?"

"Mr Hope has got the appointments all under control," Julia said. "Mrs Hope's tending to the overnight patients. I expect she could do with a hand."

Amelia found Mrs Hope in the "hotel" attaching a full water bottle to a rabbit's cage.

"Am I glad to see you!" Mrs Hope said. "We've never been this full. Can you

take over refilling the water bowls?"

Amelia took a bowl from a sleeping puppy's cage and started to rinse it. "How is the owlet doing?" she asked.

Mrs Hope let out a sigh as she took a bottle out of the medication fridge. "It's healthy enough," she said, "but there's no sign of its parents up at the hall. We're having real trouble with the overnight feeding. We took the chick home, but I've barely slept." Looking at Mrs Hope's pale, freckled face, Amelia noticed dark smudges under her eyes that weren't normally there. She felt a rush of sympathy. Then she had an idea that made her heart race.

"I don't mind feeding the owl at night," Amelia blurted. "It's half-term, so I can sleep in if I need to. I could take it home and look after it there."

Mrs Hope fixed Amelia with her worried frown. "You'd have to check with your mum and your gran," she said. "It's a lot of work …"

Amelia went out to the reception desk and used Julia's phone to call home and ask permission. When she returned, she gave Mrs Hope a thumbs-up. The vet smiled, and Amelia could see the relief in her eyes.

"It will only be for a few days, until we find a sanctuary," Mrs Hope said. "And if you have any questions, you can call us straight away. Day or night."

Amelia grinned. "I won't let you down!"

CHAPTER FIVE

Later that day, back at her gran's
cottage, Amelia led Mrs Hope through to
the kitchen. The vet had brought the owl
in its cage, covered in a blanket.

"I've made a space for it here," Amelia's
mum said, gesturing to a worktop in the
corner of the room.

"This is perfect," Mrs Hope said, gently placing the cage in its new home. "Our owl will be safe from your cat up here." She took off her backpack and fished inside. "You'll need to feed it roughly every two hours – but don't worry, you won't forget. This little one has a built-in alarm! I'll show you how to feed him before I go."

Mrs Hope took a plastic container from her bag, as well as a long pair of tweezers and a box of blue gloves. She pulled the blanket off the owl's cage. Inside, the fluffy creature hopped towards the bars, its head bobbing from side to side and its eyes bright with interest.

Suddenly, it
opened its beak
and let out a
shrill, grating
shriek. Mrs Hope
pulled on a pair
of gloves and
set the plastic
box before her. All the while, the owlet
screeched and flapped, the piercing sound
getting louder and louder.

"Wow! He really is hungry," Amelia
said.

"Baby owls live on chicks and mice,"
Mrs Hope explained. "Any other food
– even meat from the supermarket –

would make it very sick." Amelia felt
her skin prickle. She supressed a shudder
and forced herself to watch as Mrs Hope
opened the box. Inside she could see
scraps of meat with fur and feathers still
attached.

Amelia's stomach churned, and she
took a deep breath to steady herself. She
knew she couldn't be squeamish if she

wanted to be a vet
when she grew up.
Amelia watched
Mrs Hope pick up a
piece of meat with
her tweezers and
poke it through the

cage bars. The little owl snatched the morsel and gobbled it down. Then, fixing Mrs Hope with its big eyes, it screeched again.

"Can I have a go?" Amelia asked, putting on a pair of gloves. Mrs Hope handed her the tweezers.

Amelia tried not to look too closely as she pincered a piece of food. Then she held it out for the chick. It tore the scrap from the tweezers, tipped back its head, and swallowed it whole. Amelia picked up another piece of food. The owlet wolfed it down as fast as the last, so Amelia kept on going. Finally, once she thought it must have eaten almost

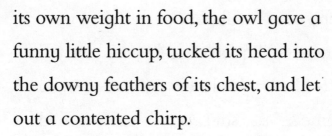

its own weight in food, the owl gave a funny little hiccup, tucked its head into the downy feathers of its chest, and let out a contented chirp.

"It eats all that every two hours?" Amelia said.

Mrs Hope nodded. "And before long it will be able to swallow chicks and mice whole."

"Really?" Amelia said, trying not to grimace.

"If it's going to live with us for a while, we should give it a name," Amelia's mum said.

"Piglet?" Amelia suggested, grinning.

Mum giggled. "He can't help being so

hungry. How about Chirrup?"

Amelia listened again to the owlet's
contented little chirps and smiled.
"Perfect!" she said. And as she watched
the owlet half dozing, his eyes slowly
falling closed, her heart gave a little
squeeze. *I'm going to make sure you do fine,
Chirrup!*

Two days later, Amelia snuggled up on
the sofa in her gran's living room with
Star, her little cat, curled in her lap. Star
snored softly, her paws flexing as if she
was dreaming of catching mice. Amelia
felt like nodding off herself. After feeding

 Chirrup day and night, her eyes felt gritty and

her head ached. Suddenly a piercing shriek made her start. Star leapt up, sank her claws into Amelia's legs, and let out a hiss.

"I'm sorry, Star," Amelia said, gingerly unhooking the cat's claws from her jeans. "I know you don't like Chirrup, but the poor thing has got nowhere else to go." Amelia hurried through to the kitchen to find her mum grimacing and covering her ears.

"Chirrup seems to get louder each day!" Amelia's mum said.

Amelia took the box of owl food from the fridge, and the owlet hopped towards the bars, his eyes bright and keen. Chirrup let out another shriek, louder than ever.

"All right, all right!" Amelia said, holding a bit of meat through the bars. The little bird snapped the food from her tweezers, lifted his head to gulp it down, then fixed his eyes on the box and squawked.

Amelia sighed. *I knew this would be hard work*, she thought, *but I didn't realise quite how hard …* She fed Chirrup another mouthful, but as soon as the scrap of meat was swallowed, the squawking began again.

She glanced at the clock. 11:00 am. *At least Sam will be here soon to help*, she thought. The phone started to ring in the

hall, and Amelia put down her tweezers and hurried to answer it.

"Hello?"

"Hiya," said Sam, sounding glum. "I'm really sorry, but I can't come round after all. Bernard didn't like what I was planning to

wear, so Mum has to take me shopping for a new outfit."

Amelia's heart sank, but she tried not to sound too disappointed. "That's a shame!" she said. "I know how much you wanted to see Chirrup. But Mrs Hope hasn't found anywhere to take him yet. You'll get a chance after the filming."

"I'll come round as soon as I can," Sam said.

"No probs," said Amelia, brightly.

Afterwards, Amelia went through to the kitchen to find her gran feeding Chirrup the rest of his meal.

"What's wrong?" Amelia's gran asked, smiling kindly. "You look down."

"It's nothing," said Amelia, with a shrug. "I just miss Sam. And I suppose … I feel a bit left out of all the TV stuff."

"That's perfectly understandable," Amelia's gran said, putting an arm around Amelia's shoulder. "But

remember, you didn't make the garden for the TV show. You made it because you really care about wildlife."

Amelia nodded, feeling a little better.

"I suppose so. And I am looking forward to watching the filming tomorrow. Maybe the show will encourage other people to make gardens like ours."

"Exactly," Amelia's gran said. "Until then, you're going to be busy enough keeping our noisy new housemate's tummy full!"

Amelia grinned. "You're right – I really don't have time for much else!"

CHAPTER SIX

EEEEEEK!

Amelia sat bolt upright in bed, woken by the high-pitched noise.

Another frantic shriek followed the first. Amelia glanced at her alarm. 8:00 am. *I should have known better than to hope for a lie-in!*

Chirrup screeched again, and Amelia sprang out of bed. She had got used to the little bird's squawking, but something about the pitch and volume of its cries set her pulse racing. *I hope he's OK!*

Amelia hurried downstairs to find

 Star eyeing Chirrup darkly from her basket in the corner, while the owlet hopped up and down, flapping his wings and letting out more urgent cries.

"What's up?" Amelia asked, standing before Chirrup's cage. His eyes looked

bright and the damage to his wing
had healed well. He looked sleeker and
glossier – as though some of his baby
fluffiness had gone.

Amelia fetched Chirrup's food from
the fridge and passed piece after piece
through the bars. But even after Chirrup
had lost interest in eating, he kept
flapping and shrieking – even pecking
at the cage bars. *He's definitely not happy*,
Amelia thought. *I'd better call Animal Ark!*

Amelia explained the problem to
Mrs Hope, while Chirrup continued to
squawk. "I can hear him!" Mrs Hope
said. "He does sound agitated. I'll come
and take a look."

Ten minutes later, Mrs Hope arrived. By that time the whole house had been woken by Chirrup's frantic cries. Amelia's mum led the vet inside, while Amelia waited by Chirrup's cage.

"Let's take a look at him then," Mrs Hope said. She opened Chirrup's cage and carefully lifted the owlet out.

Chirrup flapped and squawked harder than ever, but Mrs Hope held the owlet along her forearm, pinning his feet and

wings, just as Mr Hope had done. After examining him, she popped him back in the cage.

"His wing's healing nicely," Mrs Hope said. "In fact, I think that might be the problem. He's ready to practise flying. He really needs to be in an owl enclosure, with other birds of prey, but there's still no space available."

Amelia felt a stab of worry as she watched the little owl flap and hop. "A place has to come up sooner or later!" she said. "Whatever happens, I'm not giving up!"

"I'm afraid our time is running out," said Mrs Hope. "If we can't find a proper

home for Chirrup soon, he may become too used to humans. Then he'll never be able to be released into the wild."

Amelia glanced at the kitchen clock and felt torn. "I'm supposed to be at school for the filming!" she said. "But I can't leave Chirrup like this!"

"You can't do anything else for him here," Mrs Hope said. "Now that he's fed, he needs to be left alone. We don't want him relying on you for everything – otherwise he'll never learn how to be independent."

"Mrs Hope's right," said Mum. "Hurry and get dressed. Your gran and I will feed Chirrup if he gets hungry. But you'd better be quick, or you'll miss the start of the filming!"

Amelia skidded to a stop at the school gates and hopped off her bike. Her cheeks stung from racing into the wind, but the van for the camera crew was already there. *I'm late!* Hurrying across the playground, Amelia could see some of her classmates sitting neatly in rows

on the grass behind the crew. From her
seat beside the class, Miss Hafiz beckoned
Amelia frantically, with a finger to her
lips.

Amelia opened the garden gate as
quietly as she could and sat down at the
end of a row. Sam and Tiffany stood next
to Bernard Bloom. A fluffy mic bobbed
above them, and three cameras were

angled their way. Sam caught Amelia's eye and smiled, and Amelia gave a him a quick thumbs up. As her breathing returned to normal, she heard Bernard Bloom ask a question.

"So, Sam," Bernard said, "How did your class come up with the idea of a wildlife-friendly garden?" Sam opened his mouth to speak. But just then,

Bernard Bloom's little dog, Pansy, leapt up and started barking and straining at her lead.

Bernard rolled his eyes good-naturedly. "Cut!" he said, then he scooped Pansy up and stroked her until she calmed down.

Setting Pansy back on the floor, Bernard motioned for the cameras to start filming. But even before Bernard had finished his question, Pansy sprang up again, letting out excited yips and wagging her tail. Amelia watched the

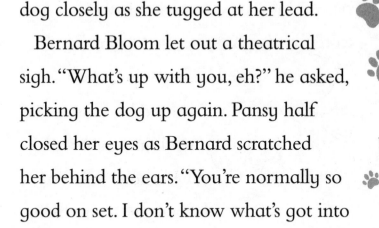

dog closely as she tugged at her lead.

Bernard Bloom let out a theatrical sigh. "What's up with you, eh?" he asked, picking the dog up again. Pansy half closed her eyes as Bernard scratched her behind the ears. "You're normally so good on set. I don't know what's got into you!"

Amelia thought she did. She put up her hand. Bernard looked at her, and she got to her feet, heart thumping.

"I think Pansy wants to chase the bees on the lavender, down there," Amelia said, pointing to the new flowerbeds. "If you like, I'll take her for a walk around the school grounds? I help at our local vets and I'm used to walking dogs. I won't let anything happen to her."

Bernard smiled. "That sounds like a splendid idea."

Amelia caught Sam's eye, as she took Pansy's lead. "Good luck," she mouthed. Then she opened the garden gate and led Pansy through.

As Amelia let Pansy trot ahead, the sounds of the filming faded and her thoughts drifted back to Chirrup at home. *I know Mrs Hope has called all the local places*, she thought, *but surely*

*there must be someone, somewhere in the
country, who could help. It's just a matter of
finding them. Before it's too late …*

After circling the playground a few
times, Pansy tugged Amelia back
towards the garden. Amelia could see
her classmates standing now, chatting
in groups, and realised that the filming
was over. As she led Bernard's dog back
through the gate, Sam hurried to meet
her, grinning broadly.

"How did it go?" Amelia asked.

"Really well!" Sam said.

"Thanks to you!" Bernard added,
striding towards them. Pansy jumped
up at Bernard's legs and Amelia handed

over the lead. "I'm sorry you missed the filming," Bernard added. "I wish I could make it up to you."

Looking at the TV presenter's kindly frown, something suddenly clicked into place in Amelia's brain. Her heart leapt with excitement.

"Maybe you can!" she said.

CHAPTER SEVEN

"Stop here," Amelia told the driver of the film crew's van. "My gran's cottage is just on the left."

It was less than an hour since they had finished filming at the school, and Amelia had been busy, explaining and making calls from Miss Hafiz's phone.

Even before everyone was out of
the van, Amelia's gran threw open her
cottage door and hurried out to greet
them. Amelia noticed she'd put on some
lipstick, and her eyes shone as if her
birthday and Christmas had both come
at once.

"Hello, Mr
Bloom!" Gran said,
reaching out her
hand. "I am such a
big fan of the show!
It's so nice to meet
you!"

"Bernard, please,"
Bernard Bloom said,

bowing as he shook her hand. "And the pleasure is all mine." Amelia's gran smiled, blushing a little. She shot Amelia a pleased look, as though she very much approved of their famous guest's manners.

"Please do come inside," Amelia's mum said from the hallway. "Chirrup is this way."

Amelia hung back, letting the grown-ups lead Bernard and the camera crew inside before following them. Even before Amelia stepped through the dining room door, she could hear Chirrup screeching away.

Bernard turned to Amelia and grinned. "Well, it doesn't sound like your house-

guest is shy! He'll make a natural star!"

The cottage's small dining room was soon turned into a makeshift studio. Chirrup's cage was set on the table, with the camera trained on Bernard, who stood beside the cage looking solemn.

When the camera began rolling, Bernard started to speak. "And now we turn to a more serious matter. While we've been filming in Welford, a sad case of an abandoned young tawny owl has been brought to my attention." Right on cue, Chirrup let out a raucous screech. "Amelia Haywood, a schoolgirl from Welford, has kindly given Chirrup here a temporary home, feeding him around the clock." The camera panned round to Amelia, and she smiled and waved.

"But now Chirrup needs specialist care," Bernard carried on, as the camera returned to him. "And enough room to spread his wings. I am making an urgent appeal for anyone with the expertise and space for Chirrup to contact the show, as soon as you can." The owlet squawked

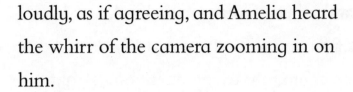

loudly, as if agreeing, and Amelia heard the whirr of the camera zooming in on him.

"And cut!" said the camera operator.

The presenter beamed around the room. "Great job, everyone!" Bernard said. "I'll get this footage sent over to Brambledown to be included in tonight's show." He smiled at Amelia and her gran, standing together near the dining room door. "And I'll see you later, at the prize ceremony. I think the whole village will be there!"

And thousands of people watching at home will hear the appeal! Amelia thought. Her whole body thrummed with excitement

and hope. Someone *must* have a home
for Chirrup!

Evening sunlight slanted through the
tall windows as Amelia took her seat in
the ballroom at Brambledown Hall. The
room was packed with familiar faces
from the village, everyone side-by-side
on plastic chairs. Amelia's mum and gran
were seated near the back, while Amelia
sat closer to the front with Sam and the
rest of her class.

"Listen up, please," Bernard said,
speaking through a microphone. "If I
could have your attention … This week's

show is about to go on air!"

A huge projector screen at the front of the hall flickered on, running the opening credits of *Blooming Brilliant*. Most of the program had been pre-recorded over the past week, but the last part would be broadcast live from the hall. A murmur ran through the room, then everyone fell silent as the theme tune ended.

People clapped or let out *oohs* and *ahhs* as the show unfolded, showing all the footage of local gardens.

Amelia nudged Sam excitedly as the segment from the school garden came on. The camera panned in on him answering a question, so his head practically filled the whole screen. Sam blushed and covered his face with his

hands, peeking through his fingers.
Amelia couldn't help noticing how
different he and Tiffany seemed on
TV – somehow more grown up. "That
was awesome!" she told Sam when
the segment ended. He shrugged, still
blushing, but he was grinning too.

"It was good, wasn't it?" Tiffany
whispered from behind her. "I expect I'll
get lots of offers for more TV work after
this."

"You did great," Amelia said, forcing
herself to keep a straight face.

Next up was the segment on Chirrup.
The camera panned around Gran's living
room, then zoomed in on the little owl.

"I'm so glad you got to be on TV too," Sam whispered, as Amelia's face briefly appeared on the screen.

Amelia smiled. "I just hope it helps Chirrup find a new home. That's more important than anything else."

"OK, everyone," Bernard Bloom's voice came over the microphone. "Get ready to be on television! We're about to start our live broadcast."

A cameraman lifted a hand showing five fingers. Then four ... three ... two ... one.

"Hello," Bernard said. "We're coming to you live from Welford, where the whole village is waiting patiently to find out who has won the most coveted prize of the week – the award for the best garden! I have deliberated long and hard, but in the end, there was a clear winner ..." Bernard paused for dramatic effect then announced, "Welford School Garden!"

Amelia gasped. She could hardly believe what she was hearing.

"I am a big animal lover myself," Bernard went on, "so any garden designed with wildlife specifically in mind gets my seal of approval! Now, would Miss Hafiz and her class like to come and collect their prize?"

With cheers and applause ringing in

her ears, Amelia stumbled to her feet
and somehow made it up to the front
with her classmates. Miss Hafiz met
them there, smiling and wearing a pretty
headscarf edged with gold. Amelia
blinked in a daze as Bernard shook each
of them by the hand. She could barely
take in what was happening. *I can't believe
we won!* she thought, while Miss Hafiz
answered Bernard's questions and then

accepted a shining silver trophy on behalf of the whole class.

"And that brings us to the end of today's show," Bernard said, facing the cameras. "So, it's goodbye from Welford, and see you next week!"

A huge cheer went up from the seated villagers. Then, as people were getting to their feet, a familiar blue-haired young man came hurrying up to the front of the ballroom, where Amelia stood with Bernard and her friends – Craig. He was

carrying a phone, and grinning.

"I've got some good news!" Craig told them. "We've just had a call from a retired bird of prey specialist named Danielle Brooks. She has her own aviary, and she even keeps an adult tawny owl. She's agreed to take Chirrup in!"

Amelia heart soared. She felt as if a huge weight had been lifted off her shoulders. "That's brilliant!" she said. Looking around at the smiling faces of her family and friends, she found herself grinning so hard her cheeks hurt.

CHAPTER EIGHT

Amelia had her nose pressed against the car window as Mrs Hope drew up outside Danielle Brooks' home. The setting sun reflected off the thatched cottage's windows, turning them gold, while the sky above was a dusky blue.

Sam and Amelia had visited Danielle

twice over the past month. Each time Chirrup had been bigger and stronger, but this visit was special. Today they would be releasing him back into the wild. Amelia's throat tightened at the thought, and she swallowed. *What if he isn't ready?* she worried. *What if he doesn't know how to hunt?*

Danielle was tall and sharp-featured, with dark grey hair tied up in a messy bun. She led them through her ancient farmhouse to the big wooden aviary at the back. Peering through the wire mesh, Amelia spotted Chirrup perched in the shadows, his huge eyes watchful.

"He looks so different!" Amelia said.

Chirrup had lost
all his baby fluff
now. He had
sleek, dark-brown
and tan feathers.
His round eyes

were framed by the heart-shaped face of
an adult owl.

"I can't believe you looked after him
all by yourself for a while," Sam told
Amelia. "He's almost fully grown!"

"He's about equivalent to a teenager
now," Danielle told them. She picked up
a small wire cage. Then, wearing a pair
of thick leather gloves, she opened a door
to the aviary and slipped inside. Chirrup

tipped his head, watching her, then flapped away, further into the shadows.

"Come on, Chirrup," Danielle said, lifting up the front of the small cage. She took what looked like a mouse from a bag and tossed it inside. With an explosion of wing-beats, Chirrup dived after the mouse. In the same moment, Danielle shut the door of the cage, trapping Chirrup inside. The young owl buffeted his wings against the door, but Danielle draped a dark cloth over the cage, and Chirrup soon settled down.

"We don't have far to go," Danielle said. "Follow me." Carrying Chirrup in his cage, Danielle led Amelia, Sam and

Mrs Hope down to a gate at the bottom of her garden, which led directly into woodland.

"We need to release Chirrup at dusk because that's when owls are most active," Danielle said. "I've been watching the woods for weeks, to make sure Chirrup will have his own territory. I think I've found just the right place."

The trees stood silhouetted against the darkening sky and birdsong echoed all around them as Sam, Amelia and Mrs Hope followed Danielle into the woods. Amelia could hear the rustle of small animals in the undergrowth, but in the deepening twilight, she could hardly see more than a few paces ahead.

"We're here," Danielle said at last,

stopping in a wide clearing, where clusters of pink dog rose smothered the ground.

As Danielle took the cloth off Chirrup's cage and reached inside, Amelia felt a strange, electric tension prickling all over her skin. *This is it!*

With a leather-gloved hand, Danielle drew Chirrup out, then lifted him up high. Chirrup sat for a moment, clinging to Danielle's fist. His head twitched from side to side as he scanned the woodland. Then, with a flap of his powerful wings, he launched himself into the sky.

Amelia watched, her breath catching in her throat. Chirrup circled once overhead. He seemed to fix Amelia with his keen, sharp gaze. Then he swooped away, a silent shadow.

"Do you think he'll be OK?" Sam asked softly.

"You can never be sure with young owls," Danielle said. "But I'll certainly keep an eye on him. Come, I'll take you on a bit further. There's all sorts of wildlife out at twilight. If you walk quietly, you might even see a fox."

Amelia did her best to tread lightly, avoiding twigs and branches. But now that the birds had fallen silent, even her breathing sounded loud.

After they had travelled a little way,

Danielle paused and lifted a hand for them to stop. Amelia saw they had reached a patch of open heath, where the last rays of the setting sun outlined the hunched shapes of rabbits nibbling at the heather. Above the heath, flitting shapes dived and swooped, almost too fast to see, making a strange, thin screeching noise. *Bats!* realised Amelia.

They all stood for a moment, breathing the cool evening air, watching and listening.

Finally, Mrs Hope broke the silence. "I think we had better head back home now," she said, turning to Sam and Amelia. "It's getting late."

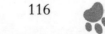

As they made their way back through the forest, Amelia spotted something in the shadows that made her heart leap. A fat, black and white shape, lumbering through the trees. "Look! A badger!" she whispered, pointing.

But at the same moment, she felt something swish past her cheek. The dark shape of 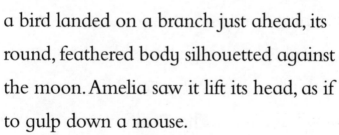 a bird landed on a branch just ahead, its round, feathered body silhouetted against the moon. Amelia saw it lift its head, as if to gulp down a mouse.

"Chirrup!" Amelia said. She turned

to see Mrs Hope and Sam both watching the owl with rapt attention, their eyes shining.

Danielle nodded. "I think you're right," she said. "It looks like he's already settling into his new life."

With a hoot, Chirrup took flight once more and vanished into the twilight.

Goodbye, Chirrup, thought Amelia. *And good luck!*

The End

Turn over for a sneak peek at
Amelia and Sam's next adventure!

ANiMAL ARK

Bumper
special
with two
stories!

The Magic Bunny

Lucy Daniels

"Breakfast time, Bertie!" Amelia said.

The Beagle puppy scrabbled at the bars of his cage, his eyes fixed on the bowl of food in Amelia's hand. When she opened the door, Bertie shot towards her, his tail wagging.

Amelia grinned as she set the bowl down, and the little dog buried his face in the food. Sam smiled from the sink, where he was filling water bowls. It was the Easter holidays, and they had both come early to Animal Ark to give the overnight patients their breakfast.

"I hope it stays sunny tomorrow!" Amelia said, filling a sick tabby's bowl with special food to help it recover.

"Well, even if it's tipping it down, we'll be having the Easter egg hunt at my house," Sam said. "My dad's been planning it for weeks. It's the highlight of his year."

"It's going to be awesome!" Amelia said. "There are so many hiding places in your garden, I can't wait."

Just then, Julia popped her head around the door. She was the receptionist at Animal Ark. "There's a friend of yours in reception," she said. "I thought you'd want to come and say hello."

Amelia and Sam quickly washed their hands and headed through to the waiting area.

"Izzy!" cried Sam.

Their classmate sat beside her mum with an animal carrier on her lap. Izzy's face looked pale under her straight black fringe, and she was biting her lip. But as she glanced up and saw Amelia and Sam, she managed a smile. *I hope her rabbits are OK*, Amelia thought.

"Is that Tulip?" Sam asked, nodding towards the animal carrier. Izzy's rabbit Tulip had once escaped from Izzy's back garden, and Sam and Amelia had helped to find her. Then, when they discovered that Tulip had run away because she'd been bored, they had surprised Izzy with a pair of new rabbits – Rose and Poppy

– to keep Tulip company.

"It's Rose," Izzy said.

"Is she sick?" Sam asked.

Izzy didn't answer at once, and Amelia felt a pang of alarm, but before she could ask more, Mrs Hope opened the examining room door.

"Izzy and Rose," she called. Then she added, "Sam and Amelia, why don't you come too and give us a hand?"

Once they were all inside the examining room, Izzy set her carrier down on the table. "Let's take a look at Rose, then," Mrs Hope said.

Izzy put her hands into the carrier, but Rose growled and scrambled away.

"Hush, it's all right," Izzy said, scooping her bunny out. Rose growled again, and kicked, struggling in Izzy's grip. Sam and Amelia exchanged worried glances as Izzy set her rabbit on the table. *That's not like Rose at all!* thought Amelia.

Mrs Hope held the bunny firmly across the shoulders with one hand while giving her long, calming strokes with the other.

Even so, Rose sat stiffly with her ears pressed back and her eyes wide and staring. The last time Amelia had seen Rose, she had been playful and had loved being held. But that wasn't the only thing that had changed. Amelia couldn't help noticing how much Rose had grown. Just a few weeks ago, she'd been quite a small rabbit. Now she looked huge, with a big round belly.

"I think something's wrong with Rose," Izzy told Mrs Hope. "She keeps growling at Poppy and Tulip, and she doesn't like being cuddled any more."

Read The Magic Bunny
to find out what happens next ...

Animal Advice

Do you love animals as much as Amelia and Sam? Here are some tips on how to look after them from veterinary surgeon Sarah McGurk.

Caring for your pet

1. Animals need clean water at all times.
2. They need to be fed too – ask your vet what kind of food is best, and how much the animal needs.
3. Some animals, such as dogs, need exercise every day.
4. Animals also need lots of love. You should always be very gentle with your pets and be careful not to do anything that might hurt them.

When to go to the vet

Sometimes animals get ill. Like you, they will mostly get better on their own. But if your pet has hurt itself or seems very unwell, then a trip to the vet might be needed. Some pets also need to be vaccinated, to prevent them from getting dangerous diseases. Your vet can tell you what your pet needs.

Helping wildlife

1 Always ask an adult before you go near any animals you don't know.

2 If you find an animal or bird which is injured or can't move, it is best not to touch it.

3 If you are worried, you can phone an animal charity such as the RSPCA (SSPCA in Scotland) for help.

Where animals need you!

 Kitten Rescue
Lucy Daniels

 Bunny Trouble
Lucy Daniels

 Fox Cub Danger
Lucy Daniels

 Puppy in Peril
Lucy Daniels

 The Purrfect Sleepover
Lucy Daniels

 Doggy Drama
Lucy Daniels

 Runaway Hamster
Lucy Daniels

 Guinea Pig Superstar
Lucy Daniels

 The Lonely Pony
Lucy Daniels

 Scaredy-Dog
Lucy Daniels

 Lost Kitten
Lucy Daniels

 Llama on the Loose
Lucy Daniels

 Reindeer Recovery
Lucy Daniels

 Puppy Problem
Lucy Daniels

 Owl All Alone
Lucy Daniels

www.animalark.co.uk